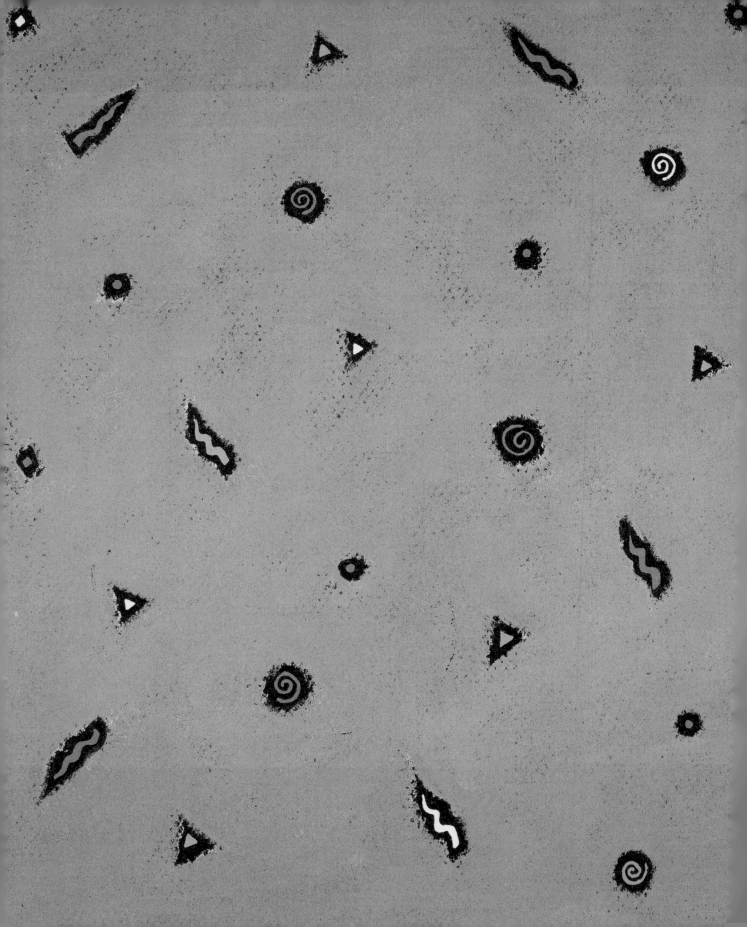

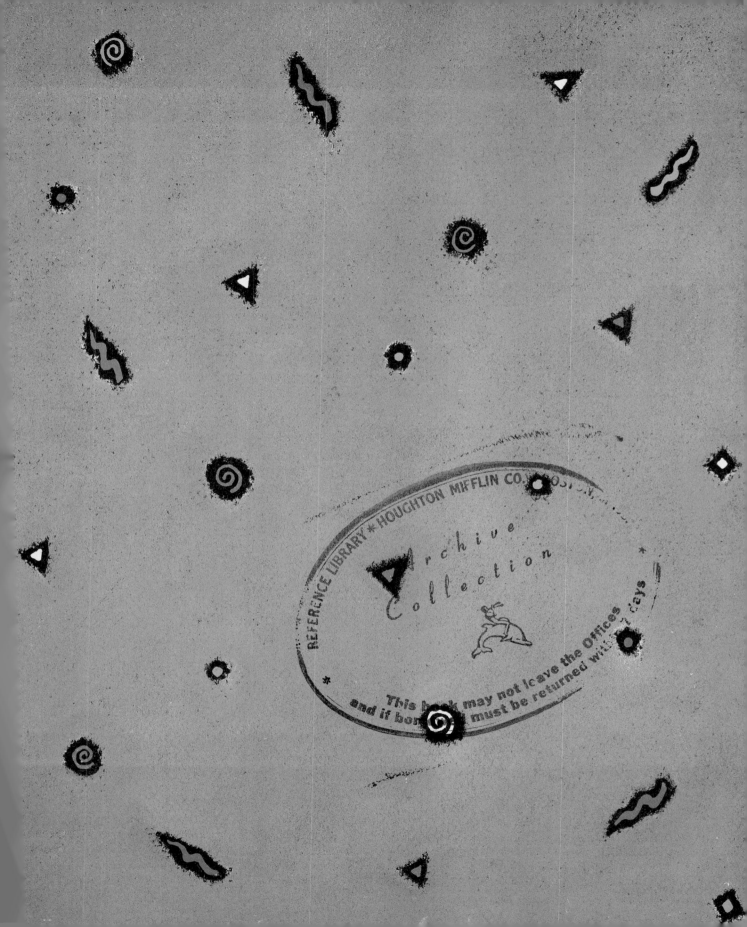

One Red Rooster

Kathleen Sullivan Carroll

Illustrated by Suzette Barbier

Houghton Mifflin Company   Boston   1992

For Sean Cody —K.S.C.

For my husband, Cyrus, and my son, Andrew —S.B.

Library of Congress Cataloging-in-Publication Data

Carroll, Kathleen Sullivan.
   One red rooster/Kathleen Sullivan Carroll; illustrated by Suzette
Barbier.
      p.   cm.
   Summary: Introduces the numbers one through ten in rhymed text
and illustrations of a variety of rather noisy farm animals.
      RNF ISBN 0-395-60195-9   PAP ISBN 0-395-70090-6
      [1. Stories in rhyme. 2. Counting. 3. Domestic animals — Fiction.
4. Animal sounds — Fiction.] I. Barbier, Suzette, ill. II. Title.
PZ8.3.C234On 1992   91-17271
                            CIP
[E] - dc20   AC

Printed in the United States of America
HOR 10 9 8 7 6 5 4 3 2

One Red Rooster

1 One red rooster went cock-a-doodle-doo

2 Two black cows

went moo moo moo

3 Three blue birds

went tweet tweet tweet

4 **Four white sheep**

went bleat bleat bleat

5 Five orange cats

went meow meow meow

6 Six gold dogs

went bow wow wow

7 Seven brown horses

went neigh neigh neigh

8 Eight gray donkeys

went bray bray bray

9 Nine yellow chicks

went peep peep peep

10 And ten pink pigs

fell fast asleep

1 2 3 4 5 6 7 8 9 10

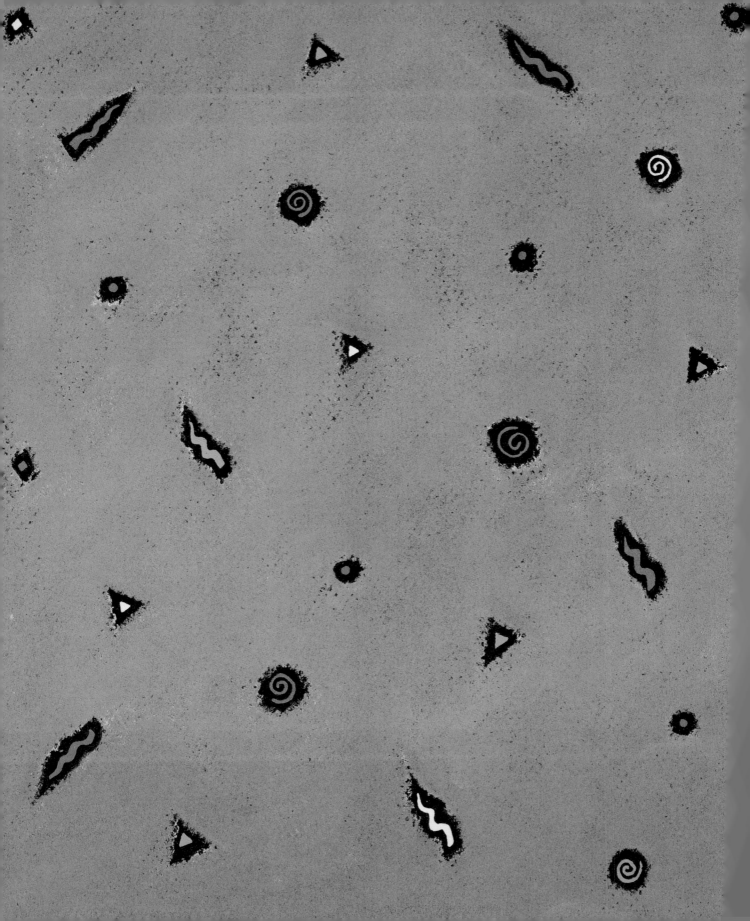